CW00420122

Copyright

This paperback edition published 2023 by Harry Thompson - Self Publisher
Imprint of Harry Thompson-Self Publisher
Glasgow Scotland

ISBN KDP 979-8-853475-31-1

ISBN 978-1-913798-70-3
Copyright © Harry Thompson 2023

The contents of this book are solely the artistic creation of the author. This is a work of fiction. Names, characters, places and incidents either are products of the author's imagination or are used fictitiously. Any resemblance to actual events or locales or persons, living or dead, is entirely coincidental.

MALKY'S
MILLIONS

HARRY THOMPSON

Jasami Acknowledgements

The Jasami Publishing Team is integral to the production of all of our titles. They are talented, creative, and hardworking. Thank you.

Cover Design

Perla Llosa Hernández

Editors

Ella Cutter
Mariya Georgieva
Shaun Mclaren
Marcus Hyka

Dedication

My family, Alison, my son Paul and daughter-in-law Sam, and of course the wee yin Dax.

Acknowledgements

I would like to acknowledge Paul Tortolani, due to the twist - he will know what I mean.

I would like to acknowledge John, my nephew, who works with me, and for his patience while I talk about (what he calls pish) which is me punting my book to customers - who are Scotland's Driving Instructors.

Finally, I would like to acknowledge Kenny Kermack who read the very first version. He thought it had potential and encouraged me to finish it.

Big thanks to Jasami Publishing (self-publishing division) for their patience and input.

Table of Contents

Prologue

Vincent strolled into Malky's office with two fresh steaming cups of coffee.

"Good morning, Boss."

"Geez Vincent - I'd get up and do the Hokey Cokey with you but I'm up to eyeballs in debts! I'm sitting here staring at a pile of bills. I've got rates! Suppliers! Bloody electricity is sky-high! Booze! Tax! Plus I've just had another past due notice from HMRC - bloody arseholes! I could paper the walls with their demands!"

Vincent stared and tried not to laugh while waiting for the explosion to run its course.

Malky slumped back in his chair exhausted. "If this gets any worse, I'll have to sell my house and just move in here!"

"Sorry to add to your worries, Boss, but McGuigan will be here this afternoon to collect the 20K we owe him."

Malky's face turned purple. Abruptly he stood up sending the chair flying and walked over to the gaudiest picture in his office. He yanked it back to reveal a medium sized safe. He dialled the combination and as it clicked open, Malky prayed there was enough money in it to pay the debt.

Pulling out several stacks, he tossed the packets to Vincent.

After a quick count Vincent announced, "we're a thousand short, Malky."

Rolling his eyes, Malky stomped over to the desk, jerked open the bottom drawer and pulling out another stack, counted out the final thousand. He reached for the super sweet coffee and downed it.

"Vincent, I really need to win the lottery!"

"Ya never know, Malky, ya never know…"

Chapter One

It was a particularly sunny Saturday in September as Jamie drove home reviewing his plans for the special night out celebrating Sarah's thirty-four birthday. Going out was not something they did every week, since they stayed in Clarkston out on the Southside of Glasgow. Seven miles from the city centre, it was often difficult to arrange a babysitter, so every now and then one of them would go out with their own friends, while the other stayed home to babysit. On this occasion, the kids were at Jamie's parents for an overnight in the King's Park area.

Jamie returned from dropping off the kids and put the car in the garage for the night.

Sarah greeted him. "You've been away a long time."

"Yeah, it took a bit longer, I was helping my maw set up the new telly in the kids' room, then I stopped for some sweets for when the kids come home. and of course put my lottery ticket on." He winked and continued, "maybe I'll keep a wee bit back for a bed picnic later - this could be your lucky night."

Soon after a taxi was gliding its way to a popular Italian restaurant on Ingram Street in time for the six o'clock reservation. Afterwards they would head out to a new show Jamie had heard about. It was one of Glasgow's finest award-winning show performed in the basement of a pub called The Admiralty Bar which was situated nearby the restaurant on Waterloo Street. The show was called *It's Enterteasement* and advertised as a *First Class Magic, Comedy and Burlesque Dancing*. Although the venue's capacity was only about 130 people, it was always full as there was something for everyone and usually had some of Scotland's top performers. Artists arrived to entertain from all over the world and it was Jamie and Sarah's favourite once-a-month treat. Jamie always maintained it was Glasgow's best kept secret.

After the short journey across Glasgow's Southside, they were soon in their favourite Italian restaurant to celebrate Sarah's birthday and enjoy some time together without the kids. Sarah ordered her usual starter of Bruschetta Ai Gamberetti and to follow Gamberoni Alla Provincial - both covered in delectable prawns. Jamie selected soup and a spicy chicken pizza. All was washed down with a half-carafe of the house wine. When they finished, Jamie paid the bill, and they left the restaurant arm in arm for a contented stroll through the city.

"At least it's dry," commented Sarah, squeezing Jamie's arm, as they passed by the famous Central Station before turning up Waterloo Street.

Jamie nodded, then made a point of stopping at the Hotel Indigo just across the street from The Admiralty Bar. It was the perfect time for a cocktail. Sarah quickly found an empty table for two. She selected a French martini from the drinks list to accompany Jamie's beer.

"This must have cost you a few bob," Sarah remarked, knowing their finances were not in great shape.

"You're worth it, babe! Happy birthday!" Jamie kissed her on the cheek.

Drinks finished, they were soon across the road and queuing to get into the The Admiralty Bar. Then they went down the small stairs to the basement where the show was always held. Another drink in hand and then shown to their pre-booked VIP seats by the very friendly hostess, who always made everyone feel so welcome. Showtime was not far away.

They usually splurged and ordered VIP as it guaranteed a decent seat, then requested the second row in an effort not to be picked on, as the show's excellent compères or the comedians usually targeted the front row. They wanted to enjoy the show without being part of it, preferring to disappear in with the crowd.

The show was brilliant and they had a great time. Jamie spent a lot on the raffle tickets, hoping to win a nice prize, possibly a bottle of champers for Sarah's birthday. Alas, it was not their night! They did win something - the booby prize 'a duck with a dick'. This was a bath toy with the difference being exactly what it said. Jamie was not best pleased.

"Forty quid down the chute," he remarked. He never owned up to being the winner of the duck. Jamie let the raffle be called again so someone else would win the infamous duck, and it worked out well as the person who won seemed quite happy to get something.

"Sorry babe, I tried to win the Champers for your birthday," he whispered in her ear.

"For forty quid you could have bought a nice bottle darling, but don't worry, I appreciate you trying."

Once back out on Waterloo Street Sarah was fumbling in her bag for her phone to call a taxi to take them home.

"Don't call a cab yet, babe, let's have one last drink across. After all, it's your birthday." They headed across to the Hotel Indigo where they had been earlier. "After all we have an empty night so there's no rush."

As they approached the bar, the girl remembered them. "Same again?"

"Yes, please!" Then Sarah turned flashing a wicked pout at Jamie trying to ooze sex appeal while blowing him a big kiss. "Am I allowed another cocktail since it's my birthday?"

"Of course you are, babe. Happy birthday!"

"Would you like me to charge it to your room?" asked the barmaid.

"Ooh!" exclaimed Sarah as she poked Jamie in the ribs with her finger. "Ask money bags here. I have no spare knickers, no hairdryer, no toothbrush, makeup or PJs."

"Don't worry, none of that matters a jot, let's get our room key."

They made their way upstairs to the room like a couple of teenagers and were soon gazing out the window over Glasgow's night-time sky, drinks in hand. This was their first overnight for a while and they were going to enjoy it.

Jamie couldn't resist winding her up one more time as they fell on the bed.

"You will just have to go home tomorrow with your knickers on outside in! It can't be the first time surely, and maybe won't be the last." He roared with laughter.

"It's not as if you're a pensioner yet." She aimed her knee at his landing gear and connected.

"Fuck's sake!" He rolled off the bed onto the floor to recover, holding his crown jewels in his hands.

"I will just wash them now and they will be dry in the morning. I'm too classy a bird to go home knickers-less and would never do the walk of shame," she announced with a smile.

He crawled over to the wardrobe and opened the door. Hanging, there was a change of clothes and all the paraphernalia he could possibly imagine she would require for an overnight stay. He obviously had planned with precision and left these earlier.

"I have a confession to make. After I dropped off the kids, I came to the hotel with spare clothes and all your stuff because I knew you would have a moan about that. God forbid no clean knickers for God's sake what if you were in an accident? You would have been known as 'the girl with no knickers' in the hospital," Jamie teased as he carefully got to his feet.

They were soon relaxed with another drink that had just been delivered by room service.

"How can you afford this?"

"Forget it. It's on the card, let's just enjoy the night."

Then Jamie's phone rang.

"Hope it's not your mum to tell us the kids are ill."

Jamie glanced at the display to see it was Dan their neighbour next door. "Hi Dan."

"Sorry to bother you, Jamie, but it looks like your house has been broken into and the police are here. Are you far away?"

"We're in town for an overnight. Remember that we're celebrating Sarah's birthday?" Jamie shrugged his shoulders and sighed. "Dan, we're on our way, be there soon."

They packed up quickly and the summoned taxi soon arrived. The ride home seemed to take ages and Sarah did not speak during the whole journey.

Standing in their kitchen, they surveyed the mess and broken back door. Sarah moved to the living room and gasped.

"They've taken everything, Jamie! How can anyone do this to another human being?"

Constable MacTavish stepped into the living room. "Sir, I won't process the list of stolen items until the morning, because I'm sure you will find other things missing. So no need to rush right now."

Jamie was looking around when he noticed that the lottery ticket he left on the worktop, was now gone!

Chapter Two

Over the next few days, they claimed the insurance and listed everything that was missing, as well as a few other items they just could not find. They also replaced the back door. Jamie forgot about the lottery ticket assuming there was virtually no chance of winning at sixty-million to one. He had never won before so there was no point in winding himself up. He just let it go.

They concluded that it was for the best they had been out. It could have been a lot worse. The family tried to get back to normal but were not sleeping well. All four shared a bed as the children were too scared to sleep alone.

Over the following months things finally started to get back to normal.

One night Jamie was watching the local news, when the lottery company asked the audience to check their pockets for a lottery ticket purchased in Glasgow Southside, as a five-million-pound prize had not yet been claimed. It showed a picture of the local shop where Jamie always bought his lottery tickets.

Startled, Jamie said nothing. In his head he was running over his memory of the night, working to remember the missing ticket. The date clicked - Sarah's birthday. Could it be his ticket? A lucky dip two lines at £2.50 each. Is this the one they are looking for? He always signed the back of the ticket so that no one else could claim on it. He wondered, *could I really be the winner? It's a sixty million to one chance of winning so no need to lose any sleep.*

Not only Jamie noticed this plea from the lottery company. Two pals sharing a flat on the other side of the city also saw it, triggering something in their hazy memories. They had been doing a little house-breaking in that general area. Also, there was the purchasing of cigarettes and a small Buckfast from that same shop. All this while they were out picking potential houses to target.

"Did we buy a ticket?" Ollie asked as he picked around the mess on the table.

"I cannae mind." Ped scratched his head. Barely five foot tall he leaned back to stare up at Ollie, towering over him.

They began to goad each other.

"Could we be that lucky?" Ped started.

"You should have bought a ticket, ya prick."

"You coulda dun it Ollie!"

"Ya well…"

Ped jumped up and down interrupting whatever Ollie was going to say. "Wait we've still got the stuff from several months back in the lockup."

"You said the lockup was empty, ya wee dick, ah told Kenny Letts we dinna want it anymore. I've no paid the rent for months!"

"Ok, quick! Let's go round and check if our shit is still there."

"I never returned the key. Maybe he's not cleared it yet."

"For fuck's sake, run!"

They both arrived at the lockup, struggling for breath, each leaning on the wall to recover. They spent about ten minutes trying to get the key in the door. Finally, it opened.

"Ya beauty!" Ollie shouted with a swift pat on Ped's back which sent him stumbling through the door at top speed.

"Ollie, all our stuff's still here!" Ped excitedly announced from the inside.

The lockup was a proper mess. Chock full of stolen items they had been unable to sell. From broken bikes to faulty laptops, shredded clothes, cheap jewellery, and a reeking stench of dampness.

They immediately started working their way through the mess, after a while Ped noticed part of an ornament sticking out from under a pile.

"There, Ollie, that's the stuff from those posh hooses on the Southside."

They pulled everything apart, choking on the dust and debris before finding the lottery ticket.

Grabbing it, they raced back home. They went through the ticket checking the numbers on a stolen laptop, and sure enough…

"Bingo! We're rich!" Ollie shouted, holding up the slightly damp-smelling five-million-pound winning lottery ticket waiving it around like a flag.

Ped waited till it came near and grabbed the ticket to check it again.

"So we are! For fuck's sake RICH. I'm gonna buy a silver Aston Martin and a case of Buckfast and travel the world! Ah'll never buy a half-bottle again!" Ped interrupted his list of spending. "Wait a minute! Does this mean 'am now good-looking, possibly irresistible, to the lassies?" Ped thought for a second then continued his dance waving the ticket in front of Ollie's face.

"Don't be stupid, you're still bloody ugly, but just a lot more attractive!"

They danced a euphoric jig up and down together for what seemed like ages before coming to their senses when the neighbour banged loudly on the wall.

"Shut up in there! I can't get a wink of sleep."

They banged the wall back. "Piss off ya clown, we're rich!"

Jig over, they sat down, slapping the ticket on the kitchen table.

"Ollie, quick, take a photo of it in case we lose it."

"Don't be a dick, Ped. Without the ticket there is no pay out - they won't pay on a stupid photo."

"Wait a minute. Come to think of it, how are we going to claim this? They're going to ask us questions like... 'why have you not come forward till now?' Or, 'where did you buy the ticket?' And what if they've got a CCTV recording of the real person buying the ticket?"

"I know we could get lifted! We could end up in the jail for breaking and entering! I hate fucking porridge! And defo no gauin' back there."

Ollie looked at the back of the ticket and spluttered. "Look! The guy's wrote his bloody name and address on the back of it as well."

Ped looked confused and after another large swallow of the small Buckfast asked, "do you think we could rub that off without damaging it? Shit, this is not gonna be as easy as it looked - maybe we're no rich after awe."

"Ave got an idea! Why don't we see if we could sell this ticket to Big Malky up at Geronimo's Night Club? He is a cert to know what to do with it - he might eve gi' us a few bob for it. He's defo gonna know what to do. Yep, we're scot free! Nae chance of porridge!" Ollie exclaimed grabbing the Buckfast and necking the bottle.

"Free money for nothing and nae chance o' the big hoose. Good thinking Batman. But wait we're barred from there for battering that bampot that knocked ma' drink over!"

"That was a whole two weeks ago Ped. We'll try the back door."

"Ya mean the one they flung us oot cos 'ave still got bruises fae that night."

"They were only playing with you, Ped. If they were serious you'd still be in traction now."

"Wit are you saying, Ollie? They woulda tortured me!"

"Naw, for fuck's sake, how thick are ya? Traction is what they do in hospital to help the bones knit together properly when you've been seriously hurt. You musta seen it on the telly. It's when you see somebody in stookies, wi' cables holding the legs and arms up in position. Sometimes ah canny believe how thick you are, Ped."

They got the bus into town and walked a few miles to Sauchiehall Street with the ticket held firmly in Ollie's hand. In fifteen minutes they were outside Geronimo's Night Club. By this time it was just after 8 o'clock, and a queue was already forming outside. So they went around the back and there, parked in the lane, was a shiny black Bentley.

"Look, Ped, the registration's M100 LKY."

"Good look, means he's in." Ped hammered on the back door.

A small latch slid to the side and Vincent glared down at them. He knew who they were; cockroaches, pond scum to be generous, the sort of criminals that give criminals a bad name. Two petty burglars with no clue, even less talent, and no respect.

"What do you two arseholes want?"

"We're here to speak to Big Malky."

"Oh! Is he expecting you? I suppose you two are here for a business meeting? Should you two not be busy smashing pint glasses over each other's heads and stealing lollipops from weans?"

A loud sound of laughter bellowed from behind the door.

"Naw, but we have something we think Malky might be interested in."

Vincent mimicked their tone. "Haud 'oan, am sure he will be interested in your proposal. Is your lawyer no wae you?"

Vincent stared at them considering just tossing them out again. Ped shifted his foot from side to side and Ollie stood gaping and waiting. It would be a miracle if they had anything he thought and smiled at the idea of tossing them out again.

Vincent gave them a full pat down then waited five minutes before sending them up the stairs

"First door on the left, and how do you take your coffee, gentlemen?" Vincent sarcastically shouted behind them while giving them the two fingers salute.

Vincent could see they had no idea what lay before them and thought, *it had better be worth his while, or you two twats could leave here as unceremoniously on you arses as the last time.*

Chapter Three

Up the stairs they went, both getting a little tense wondering if they were doing the right thing. Big Malky was known for his terrible temper and there were many stories circulating of violence being meted out to individuals that had pissed him off. His name was not even Malcolm, he had earned the nickname 'Malky' by giving a battering to anyone who stood in his way. As a matter of fact, every time a body was pulled from the canal or the Clyde Coast under suspicious circumstance, Malky's name would be in the frame.

Looking at each other they knew there was no way back and just as they were about to enter they heard a bellow. "Come in, I'm waiting for you, for fuck's sake." Malky saw them clearly on the CCTV.

Ped and Ollie shuffled into the room and stood in front of a huge antique leather-top desk. Sitting behind it was the man himself - Big Malky - probably the biggest crime boss in Glasgow. The first thing Ollie noticed was his over-white teeth, the kind very wealthy people have. He had only seen teeth like this on that Simon Cowell of X-Factor fame.

On the other side of the door Vincent smiled and thought, this is laughable, two faceless, nameless, bottom of the barrel half-wits with no real connections to organised crime asking to speak directly to the head of a violent crime cartel, what could they possibly have? Some knocked off trinkets from a big hoose in Newton Mearns.

"Ok gents, what brings you two fannies here? This better be bloody good, I charge ma time at one-thousand a minute and your first minute is already up. So not only are you two in debt, you are making this place smell awful."

Ollie immediately exclaimed. "Five million, it's five million!"

"Five million what?" barked Malky.

"F-f-f-five million pounds," Ped stuttered.

Ollie turned, "shut it Ped, I'm telling this."

Then Ollie blurted out the story about the break-ins they had done in the Southside, stealing lots of stuff, hearing about the lottery ticket and recognising the shop on the telly, then searching and finding the ticket and after celebrating, realising that they didn't want any porridge so they came up with the idea of asking Malky what to do.

"So here it is, the five million jackpot ticket." Ollie placed it gently on the desk in front of Malky.

Vincent jumped when he heard Malky shout, "Come in here, Vincent!"

Malky used a ruler to push the pink lottery ticket towards him. "This is supposed to be a winning five million lottery ticket from a few months ago. Go check it and confirm if it's genuine."

Vincent left with the ticket in hand.

Malky started typing on his keyboard, reading aloud, "How long do you have to claim a lottery ticket?"

The computer spit out:

> According to the official National Lottery rules, a prize-winning lotto ticket is valid for 180 days from the draw taking place. If the prize is not claimed in that time, the ticket is void and the prize is handed over to the fund for good causes.

"What's the date on that ticket, Ollie?" Malky barked.

"It's dated third of February an' this is the fourteenth of July." Ollie paused using both hands to count then continued, "so this ticket expires on the third of August."

"That means we have less than three weeks to claim this," Malky said aloud, but more to himself.

Malky searched for unclaimed lottery prizes, noting there was one outstanding five million prize. He jotted down the six numbers: five, twelve, nineteen, twenty-two, forty-seven, forty-nine.

Just then Vincent returned with the ticket.

"Sure enough, Boss, looks like a genuine ticket or a really good forgery. But did you see there's a name and address written in ink on the back? Must be the guy who purchased it."

Malky held out the ruler and Vincent balanced the ticket on the end of it. Malky placed it on the table and picked up his mobile.

"John, hi mate, Malky here. Can you get me anything you have on this guy? A Jamie Reddington, address is 634B Orchard Park, Giffnock. Thanks John, I'll hear from you."

Malky turned to glare first at Ped then Ollie. "Ok, you two muppets, this is how we are playing this. I need time to work out how to get some wedge - spondulix - money from this! I'm taking a punt that there is good wedge in it and I'm giving you five thousand each now. If there's money in it I'll sort you both out with more at some later date."

"But surely it's worth more than that!?" Ollie momentarily forgot who he was talking to.

Malky stood up, all six foot four inches of him. Although he was balding and over sixty, he was still a formidable sight.

He banged the table with his fist and bellowed, "This is not a fucking discussion group! If you don't like the terms, take the ticket back and deal with it yourself. Why don't you take it to the police? You might get a big reward, or then again maybe the fucking jail!"

Ped started backing away from the desk. "No, no, please, Malky. We'll be happy ta wait for a bigger payment. Whatever you say!"

"Ok, that's sorted then! Now, not a bloody word of this to anyone else. If I hear you have been blabbering your mouths off, you'll get no more. In fact, you two will be dragged oot the Caledonian Canal backwards, wrapped in quality Axminister. I'm needing new carpets anyway, so don't push your luck, OK! See them out Vincent!"

Vincent gave them each a stack, led them down to the back exit and returned after a few minutes.

"Vincent, open the windows, it's rank in here - those two need a good wash." He paused then barked his list of orders, "Take Majid and go over to that newsagent's shop in Orchard Park. Find out exactly what they know. Also, check and see if there's CCTV footage of the purchaser of the winning ticket. Finally, find out what the lottery people have told the shop owner."

About an hour later Vincent and Majid arrived at to the shop.

Majid recognised the owner suggesting, "Vincent, leave this to me, a know him from the mosque."

Vincent checked out the locations of CCTV while Majid prattled away in his own language.

Soon he turned, "Let's go, I'll fill you in on the way back."

"So, Vincent, it turns out that the lottery fraud people had been in and taken a copy of the CCTV, showing the ticket purchaser, and then they scrubbed the original. The guy gets a bonus if it's claimed, and a plaque for his wall letting everyone know that a major prize has been won in his shop. They've not told him the exact amount of the prize, but he knows they won't do these checks for nothing. He thinks it's a major prize and makes him hope that people will come from miles away to buy tickets from a lucky shop when the news gets out. He's keen they find the ticket holder before it expires."

As they drove back to the office Vincent quickly hatched a plan.

"Malky, the lottery fraud department have a copy of the guy buying the ticket from CCTV so there's no chance of us making a direct claim, but I have a plan. What if we sew the ticket into the lining of a coat and donate it to a charity shop? Then get someone to go in right away, buy the coat, and then find and return the ticket to the lottery, saying they found it and get a finder's fee."

"Nae bloody chance, that could net us he-haw. Firstly, someone could buy it straight away and it would be lost to us. Secondly, the most they are likely to give is ten thousand. Thirdly, there's five million here, I'm not letting that ticket out of my sight!"

"What about putting a tracker in the coat?" Vincent suggested.

Malky slumped back in the chair, "Nope. There must be a way of getting a larger slice. I would rather the money went to charity than get a poxy ten grand. Let's think about it tonight and meet here for breakfast and discuss our options in the morning. Ten o'clock-ish right?"

Chapter Four

The next morning Malky and Vincent met in the club's office just a little after ten o'clock.

"Have you come up with anything, Boss?"

"For fuck's sake, we've not had breakfast yet! Send someone from downstairs to go get us some breakfast rolls and coffee, I can't think on an empty stomach!"

Rolls and coffee delivered, Malky ate one roll but starting on the second, he spat a mouthful onto the floor. "For fuck's sake, this sausage is half-cooked! Is the guy from the roll shop trying to kill me?"

Malky threw the remains of the roll at the wall, leaving a greasy stain.

Vincent thought, this could be a long day, he is clearly in a foul mood already.

"Right, Vincent, this is the plan and we have nineteen days to pull it off. We are going to kidnap his wife and take her up to the house on Skye where we can hide her till this is over. Get Donald on the phone and tell him to stock up the fridges cuz he'll have a guest up there soon for full board. Not the usual type of guest, as this one won't need swimming lessons behind a boat in the middle of the night out in the Minch. This is someone to be looked after, treated well and returned safely when the time is right. Prepare for three weeks max. This should happen ASAP, hopefully today, and make sure no one becomes suspicious up there."

"He knows the drill, he's a pro. Also, Majid is outside her house now, I've sent him over there earlier to keep an eye on her."

Malky started firing questions mixed with orders. "Who should we use that could lift her off the street and deliver her to Donald in the next few days? Do we have enough clean phones in here? They will need to be changed every day so send someone out to the phone shop to get twenty under-the-counter phones, no shite and remind them to pay cash, no receipt. Make sure the phones all work and have chargers; they must be destroyed immediately after they are used." Malky paused for a breath. "How about baldy Duncan and his missus? Get them to go and hire a car. Posing as the police, they are going to collect her from her work. Instruct them to tell her there's been a road accident near St. John's school, and they are police officers sent to drive her to the hospital where her son, Sam, has been taken after being involved in it."

Malky sat back in his chair and rubbed his chin. "That's it. Put it in place for tomorrow morning. She must be approached between parking her car at the school and walking in, before she's had time to settle."

It was just before midnight when Vincent burst into Malky's office. It was not Malky's habit to be there so late, but he was busy entertaining a young lady at the time.

"For fuck's sake, can ya no knock?"

"Sorry, Boss, I've just found out something very important. I looked at the photos we received from John, you know the ones of this guy and his family?"

"Shut up the noo!"

Malky looked at the girl. "Put you clothes back on, go down to the bar and get some drinks for us. If you can find a cute pal as well, there's a wee bonus in it for you. Stand up now!"

The petite brunette got up, adjusting her dress but left her knickers cheekily on the floor. "Ok - is it still a double vodka and coke for you?"

"Naw, make it a bloody treble! And get one for Vincent! Now, hurry up, and don't get lost!"

Malky stood up. "Right, what is so bloody important? Did you no see I was getting busy?"

"Boss, sorry about that, but wait till you hear this. Jamie Reddington was in here two weeks ago with a bird. I've got photos of him and the wife, and the one he was with - she's definitely not the wife. He's playing away from home. What's more, there's CCTV footage of him getting very familiar with her in the alley behind the club right next to your motor at closing time. You don't do that if you have a home to go to, so chances are she may have a partner as well."

"Fuck's sake, Vincent, looks like he would be delighted if we kidnapped the wife! Quick, call tomorrow's job off! Tell Baldy Duncan to come and collect what he is due for his time, but tell him we don't need him for now. Leave the money behind the bar as usual."

"What do we do now, Boss?"

"Well, for damn sure, we need a new plan and the clock's ticking. How long have we left to get this done? I've spent some serious money on this now, so I need a return and fast!"

Just then was a short sharp knock and the door opened immediately.

"Hi, darling, I've got your drinks and I have also brought a friend with me, just as you wanted."

Malky walked over and stuffed some money into the pocket of her very short dress. "Thanks, gorgeous, maybe another time, I'm busy."

Malky took both drinks.

"No problem, darling, anytime, you've got my number." Her voice was low as she was trying to sound as sexy as possible. She turned picking up her black lace knickers and threw them on Malky's desk. "This is what you could have had - I'll get them another time."

Tottering out on high heels with the sexiest wiggle possible, she suddenly stopped and turned back to him, blowing a kiss before leaving with her friend.

Malky shouted, "Vincent, go and get them two hotties back up here and gee me some peace! Come back in twenty minutes, ah canny think straight at the moment, ah need sorted oot." When Malky was distracted or distressed, his speech reverted to his childhood slang.

Vincent ran down the stairs and gestured for the two girls to go back up to Malky's office. Vincent heard the double click of the lock that followed the duo's return to the room.

"Well, girls, do what you do best."

Soon, the girls were down to their suspenders and high heels, giving Malky the best double lap dance their imaginations could produce. For a while, the girls were in control. Shortly, Malky looked a very happy man, wiping the sweat from his forehead with the black knickers that had been thrown on his desk earlier.

The girls dressed up. Malky opened a desk drawer full of knickers to add the skimpy black ones to his collection. He always kept a souvenir.

As they were leaving, he shouted after them. "If you see Vincent - send him up."

The next morning was the sixteenth of June. Malky paced the floor in his office for half an hour before lifting the phone.

"John, I need you to trace a person, a girl, for me, and quick. I'm sending Majid to drop an envelope in the usual place. Get on it ASAP pal, this is getting serious. Let me know immediately after you're done. Thanks, mate." He clicked off the phone, and resumed walking around - he always thought better when he paced.

Majid waited inside the coffee shop close to John's flat. He positioned himself near the toilet door. When he saw John, he got up and went to the toilet. Opening the first cubical, he put the envelope down behind the cistern and returned to his table.

Majid continued his surveillance until he saw him head out the door to his car; he glanced at John, who gave a slight nod to confirm the payment.

Once in the car, John opened the envelop and quickly counted the fifty-pound notes, nodding at the fee. Afterwards, he pulled out the memory stick and plugged it into his laptop. The colour drained from his face. *Damn, what have you gotten yourself into this time?*

John punched Malky's number into his phone.
"Hello, John."

"Malky, I don't know what you're up to, but it just got a bit more challenging."

"Come on then, who is she?"

"Well, put it this way, you know her da quite well."

"Stop playing fucking games, spit it out! I'm not in the mood."

"She's Karen Roberts, the daughter of my boss, Chief Inspector Roberts of the Glasgow CID."

"Fuckin brilliant!" Malky bellowed and threw the phone into the huge screen television, causing a large dent just as Vincent walked into the room.

Sensing a major issue, Vincent chose his words carefully. "Looks like the shit is getting deeper, Boss."

Malky got up, pulling a baseball bat out from under the desk, and proceeded to smash the television into pieces. Vincent had seen it all before and usually found it amusing.

"Just as well that's not on tic, Boss."

Malky turned and ran towards Vincent, swinging the bat, but halfway down, he let it go. The bat flew straight through the window. He heard it landing in the back alley and wondered if his Bentley was showered in shards of broken glass.

"Vincent, better have it cleaned it up before someone skids on the glass and it ends up in the ass."

Vincent jumped up and called security downstairs, telling them to immediately retrieve the baseball bat and clean up the glass. He added. "And don't land on that because there won't be anyone volunteering to suck it out your arse."

Malky laughed as if imaging that.

"A baseball bat with your prints on it would be worth a fortune in this city, Boss."

Vincent walked over to look out the window. "By the way, you weren't really going to? Were you? For a second there I thought I was a goner! Maybe I would be waking up in The Royal Infirmary with a serious lump on my nut?"

"Don't be daft, ya arsehole! You're as near as a son to me. Remember, we started this operation years ago with fuck all, but a bit of bottle and look at us now, what a journey! If we crack this gem, we will be even richer. Maybe even think about retiring to Tenerife or somewhere, opening a wee club in the sun?"

Malky grabbed a hold of Vincent in a half-hearted hug. "Onwards and upwards, pal, come on, we have work to do."

Malky ordered two coffees and they sat down to plan the next move.

"Right, there's only seventeen days left and I do not want to leave it until the last minute. How can we extract serious dough from this bonanza that's fallen onto our laps? We need answers fast. Don't think there's anything left to do but blackmail. Let's call him and tell him we have his ticket, and we know he's in a secret extramarital relationship with Karen Roberts. Soon we'll see if he's up for a deal."

Vincent took out one of the unregistered phones and dialled the number.

Chapter Five

Jamie felt the mobile vibrate and heard the ring - the screen said NO CALLER ID. Jamie briefly considered blanking it.

"Hello?"

Vincent altered his voice. "Hello Jamie, listen to me very carefully. I have your lottery ticket and it's a five million winner that expires on Friday, the third of August, if not claimed."

Jamie went quiet - not the sales call he had expected.

"You still there?"

Jamie stuttered, "y-y-yes, yes I am."

"Now I did not steal your ticket - I purchased it from two housebreaking neds that done your house over. But I need a sizeable return."

Jamie thought *I never considered I'd see any of it - something is better than nothing.*

"Sure, I am more than happy to give a reward, no problem. How does ten thousand sound?"

Vincent laughed. "I'm going to hang up now and I'll call you tomorrow. I hope you have a bigger number in mind. Remember this could be good for both of us. Mind I know where you live, I know your family, and I know who you're seeing behind you wife's back – the lovely Karen – so don't think for a second about calling the police. If we hear of any police involvement we will burn this ticket and your chance to be rich will be gone forever."

As the BEEEEEP of the phone going dead buzzed in his ear, Jamie knew he would have to be ready for the next call.

Vincent removed the battery from the phone. "I'll throw this in the Clyde on the way home. See you tomorrow, Boss."

Jamie had a restless night.

Sarah turned over. "What's wrong Jamie? You had a bad day at work?"

"I'll be ok, just go to sleep, it's only a bit of indigestion." He was going to keep this news to himself for now.

Staring at the ceiling, Jamie realised he was probably dealing with people who could be very nasty and target his family. They also knew about his affair and he would much rather keep that one secret. *I wonder if they'd take £1 million quid? I'm out of my depth - but I'll sort it out - later.*

Jamie's life was wearing him out, grinding him down, and he knew this money could be life-changing. Walking away with four million would mean financial freedom. No more hard graft, no more seven days a week. Lots of good holidays while still young enough to enjoy them. He knew he had no option but to deal with these people and hope to find a solution.

Malky and Vincent met the following day at the office to discuss their next move.

"Ok, Boss, what are we going to accept?"

"I want half; 2.5 mill."

"So when he agrees, how will we make sure we get the money?"

Malky rubbed his hands together and smiled. "I have a plan. We're going to forge a syndicate agreement between him and you. Vincent, Jamie's your new best pal. You'll both claim the money, jointly. I've got the printer working on it right now."

"What if he then calls the polis?"

"If he calls the cops, he'll lose it all. It would take years to be sorted out in court. Now, I want you to book two hotel rooms in the Blythswood Hotel for Saturday night and get a nice private meeting room as well. Let's give him a taste of what 2.5 mill can buy. Have a very nice dinner, then get him to sign the syndicate form. Charlie will shadow you both so I can keep an eye on things and make sure there's no sign of any undercover polis."

"Malky, I hate that prick! Do I have to work with him? Is there naebody else?"

"Naw - he knows his job and we don't have time to mess about. Make sure he has the room key that's intended for your pal so he can set up some hidden cameras and bring the girls in later. Then Jamie can have a wee celebratory party, which will be recorded as well, just for good measure. Oh, if you get a chance, ask for a double lap dance fae them two lassies, honestly, they are awesome. Am telling you that it will be the best time of your life - you will ever spend." Malky smiled at the memory.

"See you in the morning, Boss."

Malky and Vincent met in the office for breakfast and to once again review the plan.

"I have two copies of your longstanding forged lottery agreement and a special pen loaded with ink that is more than three years old so it should stand scrutiny. Take them with you tonight and get Jamie to sign it, straight away if possible."

Vincent pocketed the agreements.

"All you have to do now is call him and arrange to meet him at the hotel tonight. Remind him we only have a few days left to claim or he'll lose everything."

"We will too, Boss."

"I'm havin' none of that! So, if he changes his mind during the claim, we have the affair to reveal to his family. I don't think Chief Inspector Roberts will be chuffed to find out Jamie's dipping his beautiful daughter on the side of an alley? Plus, we'll have the recording of his previous night's escapades to threaten him with if he decides to cross us. Besides, he'll come to understand that a double-cross would send him paddling in the Clyde with concrete wellies."

Jamie's phone showed NO CALLER ID. "Hello."

Vincent played his gravel voice again. "Have you made up your mind?"

"I have an offer for you now - ah'll give you one million, no questions asked."

Vincent laughed again, and took control of the conversation. "We want 2.5 million, a full half share of your ticket that expires in a few days. You don't have any choices left. The lottery has never paid out without a ticket, so we think this is a good and generous offer."

"Ok, ah'll go for that. It's 2.5 million I've never had, and you're right, it looks like I have no choice."

"Meet me in the Blythswood Hotel to finalise how we'll do this. Say five o'clock tonight?"

"Ok, see you then. How will I find you?"

"Ask the concierge for Vincent Dawson."

Malky relaxed back into his chair, looking very happy with himself.

"It's all up to you now, Vincent. This will be your biggest payday to date. It's worth £250K paid in gold or silver bars, and Rolexes that can be easily moved on. The rest will go offshore for a while to let things quieten down, just in case someone does go to the polis and they try to seize the money. In a while we can move it closer. Time to go Vincent, and put on a good suit - you need to look like five million. Keep us posted and stay on your toes, you never know what he's got in mind."

Malky went to the safe.

"Here's the ticket in this envelope, for fuck's sake, keep a hold of it. Charlie will be in and around the hotel from four o'clock. After everything's in place, he'll only call you to fix the room. After that if there's trouble, get your arse out of there bloody quickly. Finally, I have spoken to John and as far as we know, the polis have no idea this is happening. As a precaution, Majid will be outside close by, just in case he's needed. Good luck!"

Vincent approached reception to find that the meeting room was ready. He paid the cash deposit of five-hundred pounds and was escorted to the room. He nodded approval at the plush and comfortable scene. A large mahogany table set for six was in the centre of the room. Two large overstuffed leather sofas faced each other and the pictures were all muted garden oil paintings. All-in-all tasteful and understated.

"My name is Peter and I will be serving you this evening. I trust this to your liking, Mr Dawson?"

"It's great. Could I have a vodka and coke for now?"

Peter soon returned with the drink. "Anything else, sir?"

"Yes, I am meeting only one person so please, would you clear four places away? Thanks."

"My pleasure Mr Dawson."

"One more thing, how secure are these rooms?"

"Very secure. I can ask the security to call you if you have any specific questions, but they are swept for listening devices every day by our in-house team, if that answers your question."

"Ok, cool. I have two suites booked in my name for tonight, could you book me in and get me the keys, Peter?"

"No problem, Mr Dawson. I may need your card for a security deposit unless it is cash. Then I'll need a five-hundred pound deposit, that's two-hundred-and-fifty per room."

"No problem and keep the change." Vincent said handing over five-hundred-and-fifty, following Malky's advice that tipping early and generously meant you would be well looked after.

A short time later Peter returned and handed Vincent two key entry cards, informing him the room numbers were 128 and 138.

"Thanks."

"Anything else, Mr Dawson?"

"Not for now. The guy I am meeting will be here shortly. His name is Jamie Reddington, please show him in when he arrives. The girls will arrive sometime later."

"Sure thing." Peter nodded as he left the room.

Vincent quickly dialled Charlie.

"Hello, pal."

"Charlie, don't fucking pal me! Meet me in the gents in the downstairs lobby and I'll give you the key for room 128, and get the key back to me ASAP."

"That's a nice attitude for someone who's watching your back."

"Piss off," Vincent muttered.

Within ten minutes, Vincent received a text from Charlie. "The key is in the toilet cubicle closest to the door, behind the cistern. The room is all set."

Vincent collected the key and returned to finish his drink. Everything is now in place. He checked his watch, noting the time was quarter to five.

At ten past five, Vincent started getting a bit pissed off. *I feel like knocking this bampot out when he turns up. Jamie's lateness is a major lack of respect.*

A knock at the door followed by Peter opening it and announcing. "Your guest is here, Mr Dawson."

"A miracle! Show him in, please."

Vincent surveyed Jamie without saying anything, thinking, *brilliant he's about my age! This is going to work.*

They shook hands and sat down.

"Jamie, what would you like to drink?"

"A Jack Daniel's and coke please."

Peter came back with the drink along with two menus. "You can order anytime up to ten o'clock, from this menu, gentlemen. After that it's only sandwiches. I'll return in half an hour. If you need me beforehand, please dial 1009."

As soon as Peter was out the door Jamie started. "I can't work out what to think, are you helping me or helping yourself to half my money?"

"Well, it probably depends on how you look at it. If my boss had not gotten your ticket from the two weasely neds that broke into your house, then it's more than likely you would have lost it all."

Vincent put the winning ticket on the table. "Those arseholes are not the type to put it back through your door, even after they worked out that it was no good to them and there was no way they could collect on it. My boss has paid them off and worked up quite a list of expenses, not to mention the considerable time, into this."

Vincent leaned back into the sofa and continued. "He feels he has earned, or at least saved you two-and-a-half million, and considers it to be a very generous offer. Weighing up the expenses, he won't even get that. As a bonus, you'll become a friend of our organisation."

Jamie took a large swallow of his drink.

Vincent smiled and winked. "You know we are often in receipt of privileged information like major planning applications so early that we can buy up land and property before it's needed and make a killing when it's resold to major developers. If this goes well, we can help you invest your money, so there's every chance you grow your two-and-a-half million by investing wisely, if you know what I mean."

"Ok, so what are we doing then, Vincent? Do I claim the money and then pay you?"

"No, it doesn't work like that."

Producing the lottery syndicate agreement, Vincent handed it to Jamie. "This is a syndicate between you and me. Being pals we have been playing the lottery for three years now and will split the winnings between us. Don't forget this ticket expires soon."

Jamie interrupted. "What if I go to the police?"

"If you choose any other option, you could lose it all, as it will become a police matter and a court case. I'm pretty sure they won't pay out till that's sorted and then you'll make a very angry enemy of my boss, with no ticket, and no pay out. Police or no."

Jamie sipped his drink while he considered his options.

"Look, Jamie, why don't we order dinner, have a chat, and then decide?"

Vincent placed the call and soon Peter arrived. "May I get you anything?"

"Yes, we'd like to order food, please."

"Sure, Mr Dawson, what can I get you?"

They both ordered a burger and chips and a repeat of their earlier drinks.

Over dinner the talk ran to football teams, likes and dislikes. As soon as plates were cleared away, Vincent thought to move this forward.

"Well, Jamie, if we are going to change our lives for the better, we need a decision. After all, this ticket expires soon."

Vincent placed the prepared agreement on the table.

Jamie picked up the document to read it over. "A fifty-fifty split still seems a bit steep to me, but doesn't look like I have a choice. I accept two-and-a-half million, alternatively, I may meet with a serious accident. Is that how this works?"

Vincent stared steadily at Jamie, not answering.

"Those seem to be my choices. Vincent, how do I know you won't want more from me after this is over like, maybe, blackmail? After all you know a lot about me, and I don't suppose there's any guarantee?"

"Jamie, you'll just have to trust me, and more important - my boss, that this is final. We'll see you as a business associate and no more."

Jamie nodded.

"Ok, Jamie, let's get this signed so we can make the claim first thing in the morning."

Observing his companion signing, Vincent exclaimed, "that's brilliant! Time to celebrate!"

Then he put the ticket and the agreement in his case, locked it and called Peter. "Get us a nice bottle of champagne, please."

Tension released, the atmosphere improved and they started chatting like friends when a knock on the door interrupted their conversation.

Peter announced, "I have two young ladies here keen to join you both. Is that ok, Mr Dawson?"

"Give us five minutes and send them in with another bottle of that champagne."

Vincent handed Jamie the key to room 128. "Take whichever one you fancy up to room 128. I'll be in 138 with the other one. Give me a call later, remember, we don't want to be hungover in the morning."

Jamie was happy and he chatted to the older of the two girls, introduced as Maxine. She was about twenty-five with long dark hair, big brown eyes, and a bright and chatty outgoing nature. Soon, she was sitting on his knee and flirting like mad; it seemed as if they had known each other for ages.

"Let's go upstairs," suggested Jamie, taking her hand and leading her to the lift.

Shortly afterward Vincent followed.

Hours passed before his room phone rang.

"Hi, Vincent, it's nearly eleven p.m. I've got to get home now, mate."

"Alright. I'll pick you up at ten o'clock in the morning. Oh, do me a favour and send Maxine to room 138. She's been paid till twelve p.m., no point in wasting her time. And give her the room key to deliver to me,"

When Maxine arrived, Vincent sent a text to Charlie, informing him that the room was clear and he would leave the key card sticking out room 138's door.

Charlie quickly recovered the cameras and returned the card under the door, which remained unnoticed by Vincent as he was very distracted and partying hard.

Home and in bed with Sarah, Jamie wondered if he should tell her what was going on. *If I do this, will she see it my way? Probably best not to*

50

involve her at the moment and just go with Vincent tomorrow and get the money safely in my account before spilling the beans.

The next morning Vincent drove over to meet Jamie as arranged. "Let's park up somewhere and make the call."

Jamie dialled. "Hello, lottery claim line?"

"Yes, how can I help you?"

"Hi, I would like to make a claim on the five million prize from about six months ago."

"Ok, sir, can I have your name, address, and phone number, please?"

Jamie rattled off the information requested.

"Where did you buy the ticket?"

He provided the name of the shop.

"Please, could you read the twelve-digit number from the bottom? Also, are you claiming it for yourself as an individual?"

"The numbers are 5, 22, 8, 14, 9, 3, 6, 23, 5, 19, 21, 15. I'm claiming it for a syndicate of two."

"Okay. So far, from the information you have provided, it all looks in order. But you will have to present the ticket here, at our office, for verification by our security team by four p.m. today or risk it not being accepted. Also, you will need proof of ID, such as your passport as well as the syndicate agreement."

"Alright, can we come over now - say eleven a.m.?"

"That's fine sir, the team will be waiting."

They arrived punctually and were shown into the boardroom, seated at a large table with twelve seats and four already occupied.

"Would you prefer tea or coffee?"

Both opted for coffee. Vincent and Jamie were introduced to the others present by a lady called Jo, the Claims Manager, who went on to explain what would happen next.

"Just to let you both know, we will not pay out today. The ticket will need to be thoroughly tested to ensure it is genuine, in addition to the necessary background checks and setting up accounts for you both. Then, we would like to offer you investment assistance. We can also pair you both to other lottery winners who can offer advice on how best to proceed as well as plan for the future."

Jo indicated the papers in front of each. "First, we need you both to complete and sign the information sheet in front of you. This is for tax purposes, and as you are a syndicate, you will not pay tax. Due to this, we have to present a request to the HMRC, and receive a satisfaction certificate to pay out, minus any tax liability which you may owe HMRC."

Then Jo placed another set of papers in front of them both.

"Can you answer these questions, and sign the declaration that you are the legal beneficiary of this claim?"

Jamie and Vincent quickly read and signed the documents.

"Now, gentlemen, we would like to finish this meeting. I suggest a further meeting at a nice hotel at Loch Lomond called The Stags View, say this Friday at one p.m.? When, all being approved, we will transfer the money into your accounts in front of your family and friends."

Jamie felt himself pale at the thought of having to tell Sarah now.

No one noticed as Jo continued. "As a gesture of goodwill, and for test purposes, we have just transferred a non-refundable advance of five thousand pounds into each of your accounts. Please, confirm that you have received the funds."

Vincent and Jamie checked their accounts, confirming receipt of the money.

"Finally, if you wouldn't mind emailing me an idea of how many guests you will be bringing with you on Friday? A maximum of ten, please, as well as a pickup location. We will send transport to collect you."

Jo smiled and stood up to indicate the end of the meeting. "Here is an information pack with your passports. We look forward to welcoming you to the Lottery Millionaire Club very soon."

They walked back to Vincent's car, enjoying the rare warmth of blue Scottish skies. Once inside the vehicle, Vincent released a massive sigh of relief. "That was more difficult than I imagined. Well, Jamie, how does it feel to be a millionaire?"

"Vincent, I don't see any large sums of money, so no need for overexcitement yet."

Both were quiet as Vincent drove back to Glasgow, dropping Jamie at home and returning to the club to update Malky.

Jamie opened the back door and entered the house, feeling sombre as he thought *this should have been a joyous day for me but I really don't know how to tell her! What if she wants to go to the police? I don't think I'll tell her until the money is in the bank.*

"Malky!" Vincent called out.

"What happened? How did it go?"

Vincent relayed about the grilling they received from the lottery people. "They were definitely very thorough, but I don't think they are suspicious of anything, Boss."

"It's just a little paranoia."

"Funny! We'll be told in the next few days. The sticky part is that they want to present us with those large cheques in front our friends and family. I don't think my Gemma will go for being part of that."

"Well, you'll have to take Maxine and her pal, Jackie then."

"Oh, brilliant, but don't worry, I'll see they look the part - of a girlfriend."

After their conversation, Vincent called Jamie and suggested the plan.

"That actually suits me. I can't tell Sarah for now."

"Also, email the lottery and tell that woman Jo that we don't need a car to collect us. We'll drive up ourselves and as there will only be the four of us, we insist on keeping it low key."

"Ok, will do."

Jamie's phone rang the next day.

"Hi Jamie, it's Jo from the lottery here. I am pleased to say your ticket is genuine and we are happy to proceed to the payout stage on Friday. See you both at the hotel at one o'clock. We have booked rooms for you both should you wish to stay over and celebrate your new status as millionaires."

"Looking forward to seeing you there."

After the goodbyes, Jamie called Vincent. "I just had the call from Jo, they are paying out on Friday as planned."

"Good. On Friday I'll pick you up at the end of your road, from the pub's carpark at eleven forty-five so we are there in good time."

Chapter Six

Friday arrived, and Vincent collected Maxine and Jackie from the Central Hotel on the way to pick up Jamie. They were both standing outside waiting, and looking oh so fashionable he nearly missed them. No short skirts or heavy makeup, both smart, natural and elegant. He stopped, put their overnight bags in the boot and opened the back door for them to slide in.

"Nice to see you, ladies, again. Looking forward to your company once more."

Fifteen minutes later they collected Jamie and headed towards the hotel.

"Morning mate, what have you told that wife of yours?"

"Hi, Vincent, I told her I'm on a course for two days. I'll have to have a conversation with her once I've decided what I want to do. I absolutely did not think winning the lottery would cause me so many problems." Jamie laughed at the idea.

Heading north on the M8 to the hotel, the journey lasted approximately forty-five minutes. When they reached the hotel, it was bouncing with festivities.

"Looks like a wedding is in full flow here," commented Jackie.

They made their way through the large entrance to the reception desk, and just as they were about to ask for directions, Jo appeared.

"This way, Jamie." Jo took his arm and led him into a small function room with stunning views of Lomond. There was a table in the middle with the lottery signage all around and two chairs.

Vincent noticed a photographer standing by. He asked Jo. "Do you remember we said no publicity?"

"Don't worry, these photos will have your faces pixilated out if we ever use them."

Soon Vincent and Jamie were posing with a large cheque showing five million. It took about twenty minutes of smiles and more posing.

"I am happy to inform you that the money is now split and in both of your accounts, gentlemen. Welcome to the Lottery Millionaires Club! Now, let's go into the restaurant for lunch and I will introduce you to our recommended financial advisor as well as a previous winner who are both joining us there. But first, could each of you confirm the money is in your account?"

Vincent and Jamie checked their respective accounts, confirming they had received the two-and-a-half million each.

Jo led them through to a private dining room and introduced Campbell. "This is our accredited financial advisor, if you have any money questions, please, speak to him. Also, in your welcome pack is the phone number of Jane, she is a previous winner and happy to talk over any concerns you may have so don't hesitate to have a chat with her now, or in the future."

Vincent faked attention he did not feel.

Jo continued her explanation. "There is a section of frequently asked questions I feel sure should be of interest to you both. After lunch we will leave you on your own to let it settle in, but feel free to contact any of us any time. There's even a twenty-four hour help line available to you for twelve months. The details are in your pack."

Vincent nodded, still distracted as he thought about being with Jackie. He had enjoyed his previous time with her and was looking forward to getting to know her better.

After lunch they said goodbye to Jo and her team.

Vincent suggested to Jackie, "let's go and check out the room - it has a full-size window looking directly on to the loch and has a beautiful view."

He rearranged the chairs to face the loch and ordered a bottle of champagne. Soon they were chatting and enjoying the blue skies, sunshine, and clear water of the loch.

"How good is this? What a life! But tomorrow night it's back to work."

Jackie leaned her head back to look directly at Vincent. "I know something is not right - what's the deal?"

"The less you know, the better, I don't want you get hurt."

"Well, Vincent, I have a feeling if the shit hits the fan, I am definitely going to be involved. Questions will be asked, so I would rather know. Funny, I was thinking of leaving Glasgow for a while after this anyway. As you know, Malky's paying us ten thousand each for one night's work, I'm shitting myself for getting in too deep."

Over the next few hours Vincent confided in Jackie his hidden feeling of insecurity. How confused he was that he felt he could not trust Malky as much as he used to, and most important how he was to be paid a measly two-hundred-and-fifty thousand for his work on this job. They discovered they shared the same feelings of entrapment in a life that they wanted to escape from. Each found that they related as if they had known each other for years.

As the chatting continued long into the night, Jackie suggested a possible option. "I have a flat in Tenerife, a wee bolthole and I am trying to pay it off so I can semi-retire there. We could go to for a week and think things through."

"Don't think so, Malky would find us soon enough."

"What if you bargain with him and say you want more?"

"Not an option."

"Ok, then keep all the money, fuck him! We can use Tenerife as a steppingstone to, say, the Caribbean, or South America, or even further afield. Maybe we could buy a boat and sail away to wherever we want. You know, Tenerife is the closest part of Europe to South America, plenty of boats leave the island for that journey. He would never find us."

"Sounds intriguing, but I can't sail - I've never even been on a sailboat."

"How hard can it be? I know people in Tenerife that can teach us. We've survived this far in Glasgow, we can learn to sail, it can't be that hard - can it?"

"Who knows?"

In the early hours they decided to leave before Jamie and Maxine had risen. Jackie wrote a short note and pushed it under their room door. When Maxine woke and visited the loo, she noticed the paper on the carpet and read it.

Hi babes, when you read this, we will be gone. Vincent has decided to keep all the money and start a new life with me somewhere far away from here. Malky will go mental and probably put a price on our heads but what an adventure! I

will contact you when I can. Take care.
Love you, wish me luck xx. Jackie.

At the time Maxine was reading the note, Vincent was heading south out of Scotland on the M74.

"This is not the way to the airport?"

"We're not going to Glasgow airport, Jackie, we're going to Manchester. It's bigger, more flights leaving. We have to make it as hard as possible for Malky to find us."

"Should I book flights for us?" Jackie pulled the phone out of her handbag.

"No, we can't use our phones." Vincent grabbed it from Jackie's hand and threw it out the window right into the back of a small pickup truck that happened to be overtaking at that particular time.

He laughed. "There, that will cause some confusion - just hope it's not going to Manchester."

"So where is your phone?"

"Well, remember the laundry truck that was in the carpark of the hotel as we left this morning? I threw mine into the back of - so hopefully it's in a washing machine by now."

Vincent gripped the wheel. "The only problem we have now is the car. It would be good if we could hide it somewhere where it won't be found for a while, giving us even more time."

As they got closer to the airport, Vincent murmured. "I have an idea."

He pulled into a taxi rank and went over to speak with the taxi driver.

"Hi, mate, I'm going away for a month and don't want to pay a fortune for airport parking. Could you show me a cheaper place to park and then take us to the airport? There's thirty for now and I'll pay you the rest when we arrive at the airport."

"Sure, just follow me." The driver led them to a rough looking industrial estate and pointed to an entrance.

Vincent stopped the car. "Jackie, would you , please, put our bags in the taxi?"

He drove in and was greeted by an old man with a fierce looking Alsatian dog by his side. He raised a bony hand and gestured to a parking spot. Vincent parked and handed over the keys.

"Can you keep this for a month, pal?" The old man nodded, took the keys and handed Vincent a card. "Call when you're coming back and we'll collect you."

The dog suddenly started barking. "Don't worry, he won't bite."

"Doesn't worry me, if it bites me, he will be biting the wrong one - promise he will be shitting teeth for weeks."

Vincent jumped into the taxi, almost immediately aware of a smell.

"You stood in something?" Jackie pinched her nose.

"Hold on driver," Vincent stepped back out and cleaned his shoe on the grass verge. "That bloody dog," he muttered as he got back in.

Fifteen minutes later the taxi arrived at the airport. After taking the cases, Vincent paid the driver.

"Thanks guys, have a nice time."

Inside the airport they looked for a travel shop to buy the plane tickets to Tenerife. The Quick Escapes Travel was on the first floor, so they headed up the stairs and into the shop.

"How can I help you?" The receptionist was young and eager.

"We want to go to Tenerife today, please."

"North or South?"

"Preferably South but North, if we have to."

"Your choices are six o'clock Easy Jet to Tenerife South. That one costs one-hundred-thirty-two each and has aisle seats opposite to each other. Your other choice is at nine o'clock with Ryanair. It is one-hundred-sixty-two each. Also, this flight is nearly full as well, so you would be seated apart from each other. The next one you would both have to wait until tomorrow."

"Okay, get us on that six p.m. flight, please."

Vincent turned, "Jackie, that gives us just about enough time for a wee snack."

"Is that cash or card, sir?"

"Cash."

"Passports, please."

A few minutes later with formalities done, they went to check-in their cases.

"They can go on as hand luggage if you prefer," suggested the booking clerk.

"Naw, put them in the hold, I'm not looking like a tightwad that won't pay for their luggage. Next time we see them, will be in sunny Tenerife."

Soon they were tucked into a corner table in a small quiet restaurant having just ordered wicked snack food and a drink. Just as it arrived at the table their flight was announced. They quickly ate some of the snack and belted down the drinks before heading to the gate, boarded quickly and before long they were in the air. Then suddenly the guy in front of Vincent reclined his seat fully back, encroaching on Vincent.

Jackie cringed thinking to herself what's going to kick off here?

Vincent kicked the seat until the man turned. "Would you kindly stop kicking my seat?"

Vincent looked him straight in the eyes. "Nae bother, pal, if you kindly take your dandruff oot ma drink."

Clearly getting the message, he returned the seat to a near upright position where it stayed for the duration of the flight.

Jackie immediately relaxed. "Quite the little accent there."

Vincent laughed and winked. "I'm full of wee surprises."

By the time they land in Tenerife South it was dark and Jackie took control.

Heading directly for the taxi concierge, she ordered one in fluent Spanish, then turned to wink at Vincent. "I have a few surprises myself, now the first car in the taxi rank is ours."

It was a short twenty minute journey to Las Americas and Jackie's apartment. Vincent gripped her hand, his eyes clouded with concern and a voice filled with sarcasm. "Do you think this guy could drive any faster? Is he trying to kill us?"

Jackie laughed. "They all drive like that here, don't worry, we'll be fine."

The taxi stopped and Jackie produced euros to pay the driver.

Vincent murmured. "Shit, I forgot our money is no good here."

They stopped outside a high rise. Jackie's heels clicked on the cobblestones as she ran to a small office on the ground floor, returning with a set of keys.

"How come they have your keys?"

"Because they let out the flat when I am not using it. It helps to cover the mortgage."

The next morning Vincent awakened early to bright blue sunshine beaming in around the curtains. Exploring the flat, he found there was nothing to eat or drink. He got the keys went outside in a search for a supermarket. Finding one nearby, he filled a basket with fresh rolls, bacon, eggs, butter, jam and coffee. Within five minutes, he was at the checkout.

"Buenos dias," greeted the checkout girl.

"Morning." Vincent returned a smile while swiped his card, put the groceries in a bag, and headed back up to the apartment.

Vincent called out, "how do you like your eggs, babe?"

"Scrambled, please."

While he proceeded to scramble the eggs, make the toast and fry the bacon, Jackie made coffee and headed to a small table on the balcony. The scenery was picturesque, looking out over Las Americas to the sea.

Bringing the filled plates, Vincent sat down beside her. "I just realised I have fucked up big time."

"Why? What have you done?"

"I just used my card in the supermarket. Malky will trace that no problem."

He sat back and sipped the hot coffee. "I should have got you to give me cash until we sort out a bank account." Vincent rubbed his forehead. "We've no time to waste. We need new bank accounts and I need to transfer the money now."

Jackie reached out to touch his hand. "Don't worry, we'll get the bank sorted and then we'll go to the harbour. I'll introduce you to Captain Martin, you'll like him, he's Scottish and been everywhere. He runs boat trips here on the island, he's definitely able to help us buy a boat and teach us to sail."

Chapter Seven

Malky arrived at the office and punched Vincent's number - no answer, straight to voice mail.

"Where the hell are you? You're supposed to be here with my money!" Malky yelled at the blank screen.

Puzzled, he flopped into the overstuffed leather chair. Two hours and fifteen messages later, he went mad, smashing everything in sight. Suddenly, Malky felt a crushing pain in his chest and was sweating bullets.

Majid banged on the door. Getting no answer, he smashed in the door, just in time to see Malky staggering for the chair, but not making it.

Falling straight on the floor, he whispered, "c-c-can't breath," then passed out.

Majid dialled 999, demanding an ambulance.

"Is he breathing?"

"No!"

"Help is on the way, but in the meantime, you have to perform chest compressions."

Majid tried his best, striving to remember the TV advert that showed how to perform CPR to the tune of Staying Alive. In a few minutes the paramedics arrived.

"Looks like a heart attack."

They restarted his heart with a defibrillator.

"Let's get him to the hospital now."

Within five minutes Malky was lying in the back of the ambulance, with bright blue lights flashing and a blaring siren all the way to the hospital.

Majid had a shot of whisky and called Malky's wife. "Moira, you need to go up to the Royal - Malky's on his way there in an ambulance. He's had a heart attack."

"Ah him, he's been nothing but a sore heid and disappointment to me. I just think I'll stay right here and look oot the policies just in case it's cha-ching time son. Never been that lucky before, that man is indestructible. Lay odds he's gonna survive this. You go on up and let us know what happens."

Majid headed to the hospital. On the way, his phone rang. "Hello, it's Bobby McGuigan here, 'ave heard an ambulance has been called and Malky's in a bad way wi a heart attack?"

"He'll be ok. I'm on ma way to see him now. How did ya find oot so quick?"

"I have eyes and ears everywhere, see, when the auld yin wakes up, tell him I'll gie him a million for the club. He's got a week to take it and deliver the keys to us or else no deal. This is a good offer.

He's in nae fit state to run a club, so talk some sense into him. There could be joab for you in this, Majid." Just as quickly, the line went dead.

In Tenerife, Vincent and Jackie spent all morning in the bank then headed to the harbour.

"How do you know this guy?" Vincent demanded on the way.

"I sometimes gct jobs from him when I am staying here."

"Oh, aye." Vincent rolled his eyes.

Jackie punched his arm. "Not that kind of job you! I don't do escorting here! It's the likes of selling boat trips to tourists on the harbour front or running the bar on boat trips. Sometimes even running his office when he's away."

Ten minutes later they walked through the open door of the office.

"Hi, Lola, is the captain in?"

"He's over at his other office, having lunch, Jackie, just go there. He'll be happy to see you."

They headed over to Cerveza Y Carne, just across the harbour. Jackie was greeted by a good-looking waiter who embraced her and kissed her on both cheeks, before pointing them directly inside. Vincent followed her in past the guy, who drew Vincent a look as if to say this is my patch and you're not welcome. As they neared the table, the captain looked up, jumped to his feet and grabbed a hold of Jackie, giving her a lingering hug.

"Great to see you, Jackie! How long are you here for?"

"Good to see you too and sorry but not very long."

"Too bad."

"This is my friend, Vincent. We were thinking of buying a boat and going on an adventure, maybe the Caribbean or South America, can you help us?"

"Absolutely, let's discuss it over lunch, I'm starving."

The waiter came to the table and took their orders.

Captain Martin leaned back in his chair. "Okay, so you want to disappear. For how long?"

"Well, we're not sure, possibly a year."

"Do you have any sailing experience, Vincent?"

Vincent shook his head slowly.

"Well, I have a fifty-foot yacht that would undertake that kind of journey, but it would take several months to train you to sail. How long do you have?"

"We want to be on our way, a week at the latest."

"Jesus."

Lunch arrived and silence reigned for a few minutes.

"Jackie, first we need to check the weather reports, you can't leave if a storm is expected. What I suggest is you come back here tomorrow morning and we discuss this further. If you have seventy thousand, it's possible. Next, I suggest you hire a skipper and head for Barbados, once there, the skipper can return home if you feel confident, or you can hire him longer, whatever suit yourselvcs."

Jackie and Vincent glanced at each other with hopeful smiles.

"See you both in my office, say ten o'clock in the morning?"

They agreed and Captain Martin excused himself.

Later as they sat enjoying an espresso, Jackie asked, "what do you think of the captain then?"

"He seems a genuine guy and likes you a lot, but not as much as the waiter. What's the back story there? He was drawing me daggers."

"He's an old boyfriend. I guess he still carries a torch."

"I would definitely say."

"No worries, he's harmless."

After lunch they strolled back to the apartment via the bank to ask when their accounts would be ready.

"Mañana."

Jackie nudged Vincent. "Just so you know that means tomorrow."

The next morning, they all met at the captain's office.

Captain Martin was standing next to a large map on an easel. "I suggest my son Luis will come with you as a captain for seventy-thousand, everything's included until you sail out the harbour, then all costs are yours. Next, I suggest you sail to Cape Verde first, stop there for a few days so you can have the boat checked for any issues and have them fixed before sailing across the Atlantic to Barbados. Once there, Luis will leave you and fly home, and you are free to catch the wind to wherever you wish to go. He's waiting at the boat now, lessons start today, and you can leave Saturday morning. I've checked the weather and it should be fine."

Following them to the door he pointed out the boat. "She is berthed just over to the right named The Falcon."

Jackie spotted Luis and waved at him, the boat looked fresh and well prepared.

"First rule on a boat, there is only one captain and whatever I say goes. It's my job to keep you safe and teach you as much as possible. So, are you ready, crew?"

"Yes!" They replied in unison with a smart salute.

"Okay, I'll start the engine. Jackie, you cast off the stern and roll the rope up, making sure it's properly stored on the deck. Vincent, you cast off the bow rope, jump on board and do the same, make sure the rope is stored away securely. If you drop the rope in the water, it could go under the boat and get tanglcd in the prop, rendering our engine useless. So this just can't happen and is rule number two. After that lift the fenders into the boat, they are on each side to protect the vessel when we are alongside a pontoon or another boat."

After a day's sailing they returned to the harbour tired, aching and thirsty. They thanked Luis and head back to Jackie's flat.

"Jackie, this needs to be our last night here in the flat, the next few nights we should spend on the boat. It's a good idea for two reasons, first to get used to it, and second just in case your flat has been compromised."

After breakfast they packed their bags, tidied the flat and handed the keys to the concierge before heading to the harbour. Climbing aboard Vincent started to feel the pressure a bit, *we are sailing thirty to forty miles in a day practicing and soon they will undertake a journey of eight-hundred miles to Cape Verdy then another two thousand four hundred miles to Barbados that's at least eight days constant sailing day and night for your first sail, it's exciting and scary at the same time but I'm saying nothing to worry Jackie.*

Luis appeared at the harbour side and started his orders. "Ok cast off."

Soon they were out at sea and he plotted a practice course for Cape Verdy. They all seemed to be getting on well, Jackie and Vincent were learning quickly.

"Before we start today do you have any questions Vincent? Jackie?"

"What if one of us falls in?" Jackie asked.

"Ah, good question. Man overboard! Once at sea in earnest, we'll trail a long special floating rope behind us. If you fall in, swim to back of the boat and try to catch that first, because by the time we drop the sail and turn round you could be a good bit away, and out of sight. As soon as someone is overboard the drill is to throw the lifebelt in immediately. This will float in the same direction as the person in the water but will be seen as it has the aerial with a flag. If you are in the water and miss the rope, try to get to the lifebelt. We'll definitely practice this manoeuvre tomorrow so you are both familiar with it."

After another long day they returned to the harbour and berthed the boat for the night.

"I'm off home see you both about ten-ish tomorrow."

Vincent ordered two pizzas. "We might as well have a wee treat won't be able to do this after tomorrow."

They spent the next two days out in the waters off the Canary Islands and ensured that all preparations were completed so they were ready to leave on the Saturday.

The next morning Vincent opened the curtains and immediately noticed a black minibus with dark windows parked in the harbour near the boat. His heart sank he knew something was wrong.

"Jackie, wake up babe. You need to leave the boat. Head to Captain Martin's office."

Jackie looked up at Vincent. "Whatever happens, I'm in it with you." She brushed his lips with a quick kiss and left.

The driver got out and approached the boat. "Vincent, I have someone who wants to talk to you can you follow me please?"

As Vincent strolled toward the vehicle, his brain was racing. Will he kidnap me and return me to the UK? Or worse?

The driver pulled the van door open and inside behind the table sat Big Malky looking pale and a bit thinner but just as intimidating.

"We need to talk Vincent."

Vincent took the seat opposite Malky. "I suppose you want me to return the money Boss? Where will I be then? You know, I just wanted a better life - it's been tough between us lately. So I just took a chance. By the way how did you find us?"

"One thing at a time! I had a bloody heart attack, a heart bypass, and just ma luck too auld to qualify for a mobility motor."

Malky sat back and took a deep breath. "I know it's been different between us and there is a reason for that, I'll tell you in a minute." He took another breath and continued. "Ave sold the club to McGuigan and Majid is in charge there now. I'm not here for revenge. That's the furthest from my mind I'm here to put the cards on the table and tell you the reason it's been so tough lately."

Vincent stared at Malky his heart pounded so much he wondered if he was going to have a heart attack.

"I should have told you a while ago, Vincent... I'm your Da."

"You're me Da?"

"I knew straight away when you came to the club for a job. You see I dated the lovely Jenny over forty-odd years ago. I didn't tell anyone else. No one knows 'cause you coulda been used to get at me in Glasgow. So it was for the best."

Malky pulled a long drink from the glass on the table. "I know you're busy and I don't want to keep you back from your sailing practice but can you bring Jackie for dinner tonight? I'm staying in the Hotel Sunshine over on the beach."

Vincent continued to sit and stare just speechless. He had gone from being an orphan to having a father in one little second.

"Vincent, I would like to spend some time with you both and chat more before you sail off on Saturday. If that's still the plan? Now you know you don't have to run. Is seven okay? I'll send the minibus to pick you up."

Malky leaned back and laughed. "I would ask you if you needed any money but you've got it all."

Vincent had still not said a word. He got out of the van when Malky followed him and gave him a clumsy hug.

"I've a bit to think about, Boss... Da."

He watched Malky get back into the van and as it pulled away.

Jackie and Luis were watching from across the harbour and both ran to Vincent.

Jackie put her hand on Vincent's arm. "What's going on? Are you okay?"

Vincent shook his head still in shock. "Sorry Luis can you give us an hour. We've just had a visitor and it appears we don't have to make ourselves scarce."

"Jackie, we need to talk about how to proceed."

Vincent quickly relayed the shocking reveal to Jackie.

"Vincent let's just continue with the training today until we speak to Malky tonight, and then we can see where we fit in to his plans."

"Come on now, time for today's practice." Commanded Luis.

A full day of practice, they returned to the harbour and were ready by seven for the minibus to pick them up. Inside they headed to the restaurant where Malky waited alone at the table. He stood with the help of a stick and hugged them both.

"Sit down and listen to what I have to say," Malky ordered.

A bottle of champagne arrived and they took a few minutes for the popping of the cork, serving, and toasting.

"Now you know I'm not one for small talk. I have found a business opportunity and have just made an offer to purchase a farm on the outskirts of Glasgow."

"A farm boss… I mean Da what do we know about farming?"

"All we need to know is that this farm has a massive hollow that should be refilled as the material has been removed, so it should be a shoe-in for planning permission, and should bring in a few million. Also, there's a house to be renovated. So basically, reinstate the ground with infill charged at thirty-five quid a load. I think it will be a good wee earner."

Malky leaned back to sip his glass then leaned forward again. "Get plans to remodel the house and convert several barns into houses. Even on the back of a napkin this looks a good earner, then when it's finished we can stick wind turbines on it and retire. What do you think? Are you in?"

Jackie was sitting back just sipping the champaign, watching them both, and waiting for Vincent's reaction.

"Well, it's a lot to take in. Let us think about it and speak tomorrow after our last sailing lesson. How does that sound?"

"Sure let's catch up tomorrow."

The next day was spent again out in the waters off The Canary Islands. Both beginning to feel like sailors, although there was still a lot to learn all preparations were done and they were now prepared to leave on the Saturday morning

Before he left the boat on the Friday night Luis extended an invitation. "My dad has reserved a table at Cerveza Y Carne for seven o'clock tonight and you are both invited. But I don't recommend you overdo it as tomorrow will be a long day, we leave at six in the morning - sharp."

They both decided to have their last proper shower at the harbour shower block and a final stroll on dry land around Las Americas before meeting Captain Martin for dinner.

Seated through the back, Vincent could see the waiter watching him, making him feel a bit nervous almost like he's hoping for failure.

"How's the new sailors doing - got over the sea sickness yet?" asks Captain Martin.

"Not really bothered us much." Jackie's smile was a bit brighter.

"Thank you for transferring the seventy thousand to my account, and here is your bill of sale. Keep this as you may be asked for proof of ownership."

The food began to arrive and the conversation in full swing discussing a variety of saving stories. Vincent felt the hairs on the back of his neck start to itch, he looked around to check on the waiter and standing six feet away was the unmistakable figure of Big Malky who gestured to Vincent to come outside. Sitting at a vacant table outside Vincent paused and then headed outside.

"Ok partner, you in? Or out?"

Vincent leaned over and hugged Malky. "We're in Dad. Geez, I didn't even stutter out b-b-boss that time. Though I do think it will take a while to get used to calling you Dad. I've bought the boat now and we are due to leave for a trip to Barbados in the morning, and should be away for about two months."

"Nae bother! You crack on with leaving in the morning."

"We'll return and fill you in on our adventures now that we have a lot of time to chat? Ahead I mean."

"That we do! One more thing, and something else 'ave been speaking to your old pal Jamie Reddington. Guess what? He's divorcing his wife and is going to start a new life with his bird, and is interested in investing in our new venture. Now let's go inside and have something to eat."

Vincent walked back to the table in the restaurant announcing. "Hi all! I would like you to meet my dad."

At nine o'clock the captain ended the party. "I have an early rise in the morning to see off my friends off so I am turning in early see you all harbour side tomorrow morning six o'clock in the morning. Goodnight."

Vincent walked Malky back to his hotel and they shook hands just outside. "Enjoy your adventure son, it's a long way from Glasgow's shite weather, see you soon."

"Will do - and a couple months is not long."

The following morning Luis arrived at five and chapped on the cabin door. "Wakey! Wakey! We need breakfast and to take on drinking water before our six o'clock start."

At six they were ready to cast off. Just in time the captain and Malky turned up to wave them off.

Malky handed Vincent a box.

"What's this da? No room for any unnecessary stuff."

"It's a satellite phone so no reason not to keep in touch! Have a good trip! And we'll speak soon."

Malky turned and gave a hug. "Bye Jackie."

The ropes were cast off and they motored slowly out of the harbour into the open sea looking the part. The sails were up, and Malky watched the boat get smaller and smaller until it was completely out of sight.

The Raven

It's the Dream

Glaswegian Dialect Dictionary

'ave -	I have
A few bob -	expensive
ah -	I
auld -	old
aye -	yes
bampot -	idiot
Buckfast -	known as Bucky
Bucky	-fortified wine with caffeine
burd -	woman
canny -	can't/shrewd/sharp
cert -	certainty/certain
cos -	because
da -	dad
defo -	definitely
dinna -	didn't
eve -	even
fae -	from
gauin' -	going
gee -	give
gi' -	give
gonna -	going to
haud 'oan -	hold on
he-haw -	nothing
heid -	head
hooses -	houses
I cannae mind	I can't remember
joab -	job/employment
knickers -	lingerie/underwear

lassies -	girls
ma' -	my or mother (context)
Maw -	mom
nae -	no
naebody -	nobody
naw -	no
o' -	of
on tic -	debt to be paid
oot -	out
pal -	friend
polis -	police
quid -	pound
scot free -	to get away with something
stooky -	plaster cast for broken bone
ta -	to/thank you (context)
telly -	TV
the noo -	now
tight wad -	scrooge/penny pincher
tookies -	multiple plaster casts
twa -	two
wae -	with
weans	children
wee -	small/ a little
wi -	with
wit -	what
woulda -	would have
ya -	you/yes
yin -	one
You coulda dun it -	You could have done it

About The Author

Harry Thompson was born in Glasgow in 1958, and did not take to education, preferring to leave school as soon as possible starting work at sixteen. On the 'tools' all his life he had no idea he could (or would) write a book, pen poetry, or even write jokes,

Turning sixty and entering lockdown he used the downtime to write this novella, as it had been developing in his head for years. Now this story (as Harry likes to say) will see the light of day thanks to the Self-Publishing division of Jasami Publishing Ltd.

He also loves stand-up comedy and can be found at various events around Scotland. Check out his Instagram: harrytcomedian for up-to-date event details.

Malky's Millions

Harry Thompson

Malky's Millions

Harry Thompson

Malky's Millions

Printed in Great Britain
by Amazon